TWOgether

Susan Gal

 Nancy Paulsen Books

Hey, let's see
if someone wants to
play with me . . .

Well,
I cannot play
with you.

I do not
need TWO to do
what I do.

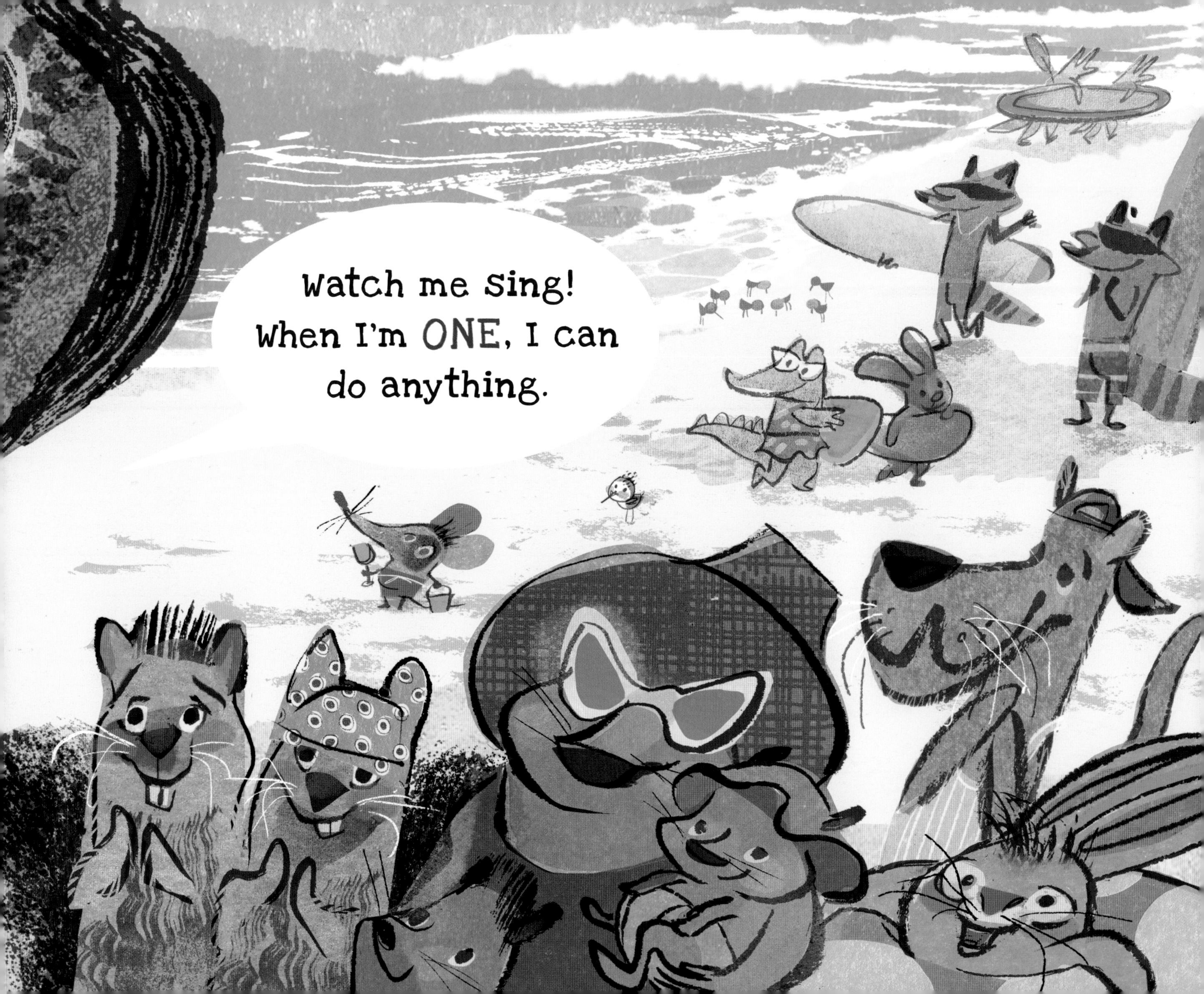
Watch me sing! When I'm ONE, I can do anything.

So why
is TWO better
than ONE?

Watch, and I'll show you what TWO can do!

TWO makes the seesaw go up and down.

TWO keeps our beach ball flying around.

Hey! If **TWO** is better than **ONE**, what about **THREE**?

Now add
one more,
and we have
FOUR!

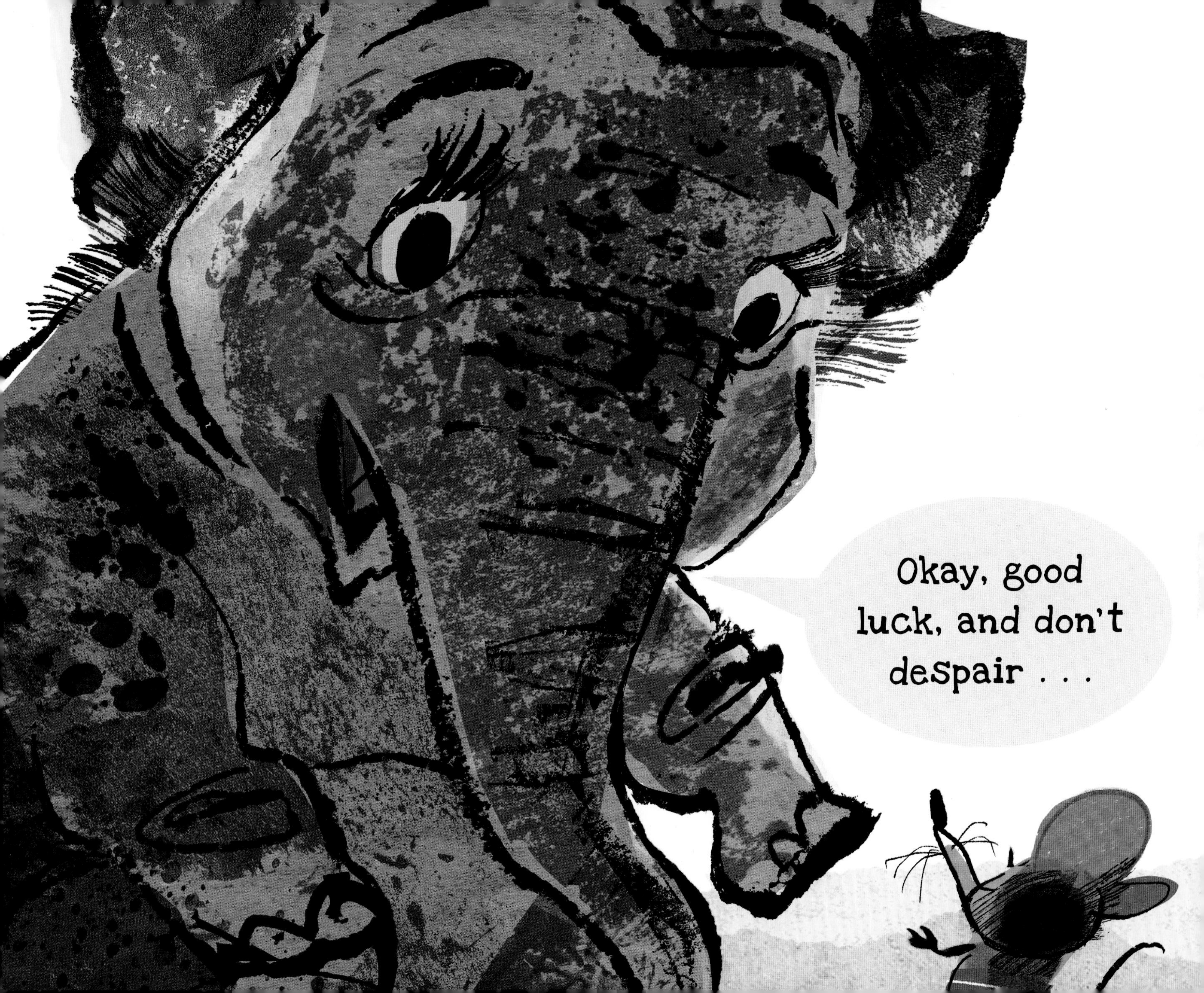
Okay, good luck, and don't despair . . .

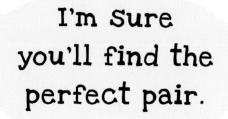

I'm sure you'll find the perfect pair.

Hi! Would you
like to play with me?
TWO's more fun,
do you agree?

TWOgether is my favorite way!

For Bug

NANCY PAULSEN BOOKS
An imprint of Penguin Random House LLC, New York

Nancy Paulsen Books is a trademark of Penguin Random House LLC.

Visit us online at penguinrandomhouse.com

Library of Congress Cataloging-in-Publication Data
Names: Gal, Susan, author. | Title: Twogether / Susan Gal.
Description: New York: Nancy Paulsen Books, [2021] | Summary: "A lonely shrew wants a friend to play 'twogether' with as a pair,
but Elephant thinks it's more fun to play either by herself or in a big group"-Provided by publisher.
Identifiers: LCCN 2020018377 | ISBN 9781984812919 (hardcover) | ISBN 9781984812926 (ebook) | ISBN 9781984812933 (ebook)
Subjects: CYAC: Play-Fiction. | Counting-Fiction. | Friendship-Fiction.
Classification: LCC PZ7.G12964 Tw 2021 | DDC [E]-dc23
LC record available at https://lccn.loc.gov/2020018377

Manufactured in China by RR Donnelley Asia Printing Solutions Ltd.
ISBN 9781984812919
1 2 3 4 5 6 7 8 9 10

Design by Suki Boynton · Text set in Love Ya Like a Sister Solid
The illustrations were rendered in pencil and ink and assembled digitally.

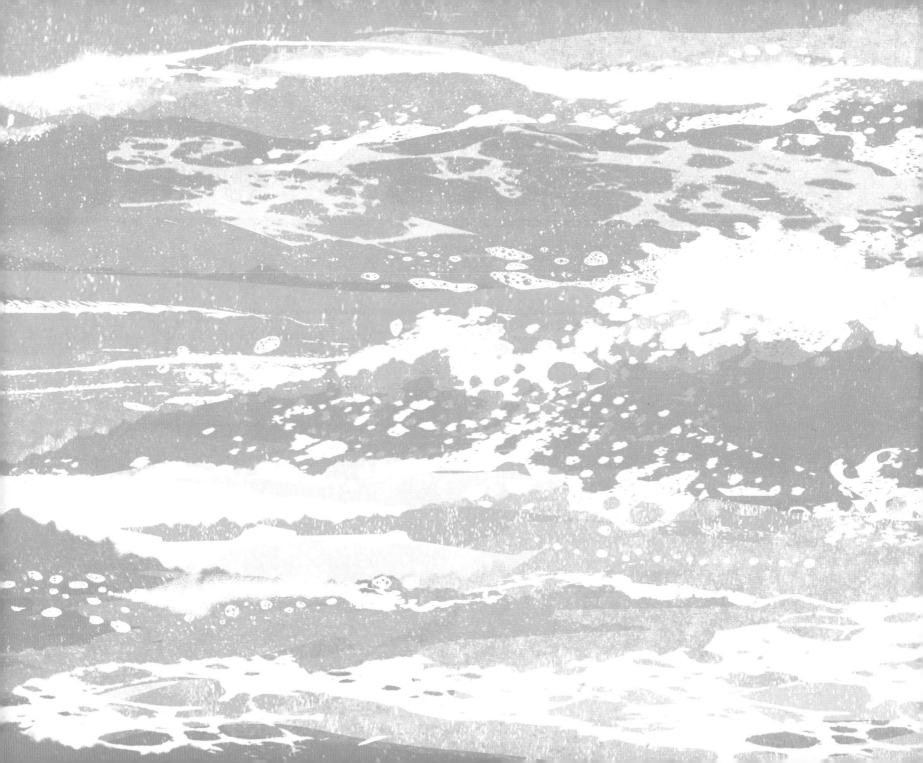

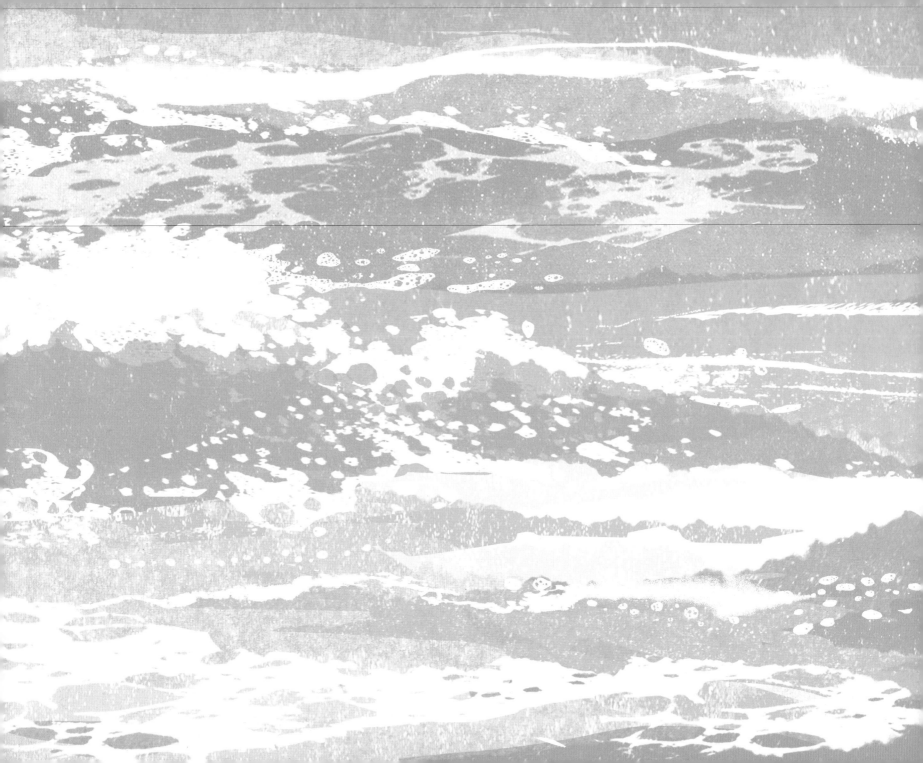